FURTHERMORE

The Seamus McCree Series
By James M. Jackson

NOVELS

Ant Farm
Bad Policy
Cabin Fever
Doubtful Relations
Empty Promises
False Bottom
Granite Oath
Hijacked Legacy

NOVELLAS

Furthermore
Low Tide at Tybee

NONFICTION
By Jim Jackson

One Trick at a Time:
How to Start Winning at Bridge

FURTHERMORE

A Seamus McCree Novella

James M. Jackson

First Edition
Trade Paperback Edition: April 2020

Wolf's Echo Press
PO Box 54
Amasa, MI 49903
www.WolfsEchoPress.com

This is a work of fiction. Any references to real places, real people, real organizations, or historical events are used fictitiously. Other names, characters, organizations, places, or events are the product of the author's imagination.

ISBN-13 Trade Paperback: 978-1-943166-20-6
ISBN-13 Electronic   978-1-943166-19-0

Printed in the United States of America
1098765432

DEDICATION

For all the readers who wanted to know.

ONE

EMBRACING THE BURN IN MY shoulders, I counted repetitions under my breath. At twenty, I released the pull bar from the universal gym and opened my eyes to discover my ex-wife appraising me, a crooked smile on her face. I pulled off my headphones. Eric Clapton's "Layla" spilled tinnily into the room.

"Sorry to interrupt," Lizzie said. "How did today's rehab go?"

"She's a latter-day Marquis de Sade. Boy howdy, that girl can bring me to tears. She—"

"You don't fool me, Seamus McCree—a.k.a. Mister No-Pain-No-Gain. Besides, you love watching her cute ass sashay around."

"Lizzie, she's younger than Paddy."

"Which is why she still has a cute ass. Speaking of our son, he took Megan to her play date and by now should be rowing on the Charles. He promises to be back in time to take you to your mysterious lunch appointment. I'm heading for my ten-thirty meeting with the mayor. No headphones, Seamus. You need to hear the real estate agent when he arrives."

"He knows to ring the downstairs bell?"

"Should, but just in case, I left the upstairs door open so you can hear." She gestured to the oak door that closed off the top of the grand interior staircase, added during her conversion of the Cambridge, Massachusetts Victorian house into upstairs and downstairs condos.

"He's scheduled for eleven, but it will depend on how long they take at their earlier stops. He knows you'll be here. Keep out of their way and it'll be fine." She placed her hands on her hips and arranged her face to appear stern. "And don't overdo it and tear a muscle or something."

"Yeah . . . yeah . . . yeah," I said. "You sound just like a wife."

"Oh lord, save me." She swatted my shoulder. "Been there. Done that. I'm off." She waved a toodle-oo over her shoulder and performed an exaggerated sashay to the front door, the tapping of her low heels echoing off the plaster walls of the sparsely furnished room. Lizzie may have been thirty years older than my physical therapist, but she kept herself in good shape. Her ass still looked fine. But truth be told, I've always been more a leg than a butt man.

I silenced the mp3 player and toweled off the equipment. Lizzie was right about not overdoing it. Less than four weeks earlier, I had destroyed my ankle while capturing someone who had tried to kill me. Lizzie had generously offered to let me stay in the first-floor condo she had recently put on the market: I wouldn't have to rehab in an overheated nursing home, and Paddy could stay with her upstairs to help take care of me. As a bonus, three-year-old Megan got to tag along with her father and visit her grandparents.

Should I take a quick shower before the potential buyer arrived and chance being caught *au naturel* or wait until after their visit and possibly run out of time before leaving with Paddy for lunch?

The buzz of the condo's old-fashioned doorbell resolved my dilemma. I grabbed crutches and looked around to make sure I didn't need to straighten anything before I let in the prospective buyer. The open-concept living/dining room contained a table with four chairs—tucked in, two lounge chairs with lamps—shades straight, and the universal gym Paddy had rented for me. I pictured the bedroom: bed made, pile of books on the nightstand, not the floor. Bathroom clean. Breakfast dishes in the drainer. The remaining rooms were empty.

I sniffed my armpits. Sweaty, but okay. The easiest place to store the towel was around my neck. I crutched to the door and peered through the side windows. Man and woman. The guy looked like he played middle linebacker in college: six-footer and solid. His suit and tie seemed odd for a real estate agent these days. Well, maybe agents who showed seven-figure properties dressed differently. The woman buyer stood partially hidden behind him. I sensed sharp angles hidden by a deep-blue pants suit.

Remembering to put a smile on my face and in my voice, I opened the door and said, "You're earlier than I expected. I'll escape to the patio while you check the place out. Okay?"

The guy's face scrunched in confusion. The woman stepped around him and held out a badge case. "FBI, Mr. McCree. I'm Special Agent Grozniak. We'd like a few minutes of your time. May we come in?" She offered her hand.

My mouth went Sahara Desert dry. My stomach clenched. Beads of perspiration popped onto my forehead. *Oh, shit. What did they find?*

Her handshake was firm and contrasted with the limp one I received from her partner, Special Agent Unger, who smelled of cheap aftershave lotion. I waved them toward the table and closed the door behind them. *Try not to lie, Seamus. They throw you in jail for that.* With deliberation, I took a seat and balanced the crutches against the fourth chair. The agents gave the impression they had all the time in the world. "How can I help you?" I asked, knowing full well I would try hard to hinder their investigation if they were here for the reasons I thought.

Agent Grozniak took the lead. "Have you kept in touch with John Smith, the self-styled Happy Reaper?"

His name is John Smith? You've got to be kidding. Her question seemed to imply the Happy Reaper and I had something of a relationship. Less than a month ago I had caught the professional assassin. He now waited in jail for various states and the federal government to decide who would prosecute him first. The FBI could access visitor logs and phone records to know I'd had no contact with him since his arrest. What subtext was I missing?

"It's a simple question," she said.

"I've never been in touch with him. Our paths have crossed several times."

"Then can you explain why he placed you on his visitor's list?"

"I was unaware of that." *What the hell was he up to?*

"His list includes a bevy of lawyers and three McCrees: you, your mother, and your son. Curious, don't you think? We're starting with you. Why would he do that?"

I had no idea and told her so. The Happy Reaper and I first crossed paths nine years ago. He had been at the top of his profession, earning six-figure payments for his work. "I was heading the financial crimes unit of Criminal

Investigations Group when I first met him. You familiar with them—an international not-for-profit local police can call in to provide free expertise? Anyway, I foiled a mass-murder plot that would have earned him millions. The second time was years later. I was helping my professional bodyguard partner protect a federal witness who the defendants had hired the Happy Reaper to eliminate. We got the guy into federal custody. Before our client testified, the Happy Reaper killed him . . ." The words caught in my throat. ". . . and my partner. I assume you know about last month. I had him in custody. He tried to escape. I shot him."

"I've reviewed the files relating to that day," Agent Grozniak said. "Something stinks, Mr. McCree, and everyone—local cops, state cops—seem to have Vicks VapoRub stuck up their noses. Why do you think Smith insists he was there because your mother hired him to protect you from someone trying to kill you? You know, the other guy you captured—the one who screwed up your ankle?"

"A crafty ploy. If I didn't let him go, he said he'd cause our family grief with that accusation. He's succeeding. You guys are here, right? He's in jail with no hope of ever getting out and entertaining himself by making mischief."

"Then why do you think he was there?"

I shrugged—a response that wouldn't bring me jail time for lying.

She rubbed her eyes, something I did if I wanted time to think. With me it meant pushing up my glasses. If she was myopic, she wore contacts. I risked a quick look in Agent Unger's direction. He maintained an interested smile and nodded at my glance. Police use silence to encourage people to talk. I can do silence like a monk. Agent Grozniak broke first.

"Mr. Smith claims that, after you shot him, you lifted the keys to his Airbnb and stole a bunch of stuff." She checked her notes. "A laptop and the money your mother paid him for a down payment. We confirmed that during Mr. Smith's stay, his apartment's Wi-Fi carried traffic, upload and download using an encrypted browser. Unfortunately, we can't tell what that traffic was. Did you take those items, Mr. McCree?"

"No." Technically the truth; Paddy had taken them.

"A jailhouse snitch told us Smith used an illicit phone to send text messages. Did he send any to you?"

A tingle of fear ran down my spine. The Happy Reaper had threatened to kill everyone associated with his arrest once he escaped prison. Had he given up on escaping and was texting to arrange for someone else to murder us?

"Why would you even ask?" I responded.

"Because in interviews, the only thing he will talk about is your family. May we have permission to access your phone records?"

The problem with my phone records was not nonexistent texts from the Happy Reaper. Unless Paddy had used his extralegal hacking skills to erase my phone's location data, the records would prove I had been in the vicinity of the Happy Reaper's Airbnb. Paddy had used the Happy Reaper's key and taken the money, the laptop, and other items that incriminated my seventy-nine-year-old mother. She *had* hired the Happy Reaper to do away with the other guy trying to kill me.

I'd need a book to explain the convoluted business but saying anything was only asking to hang myself or my family. It was time to call their bluff. "I'm not a fan of governments spying on their citizens. If you really think the Happy Reaper and I are in contact, get a warrant. Is there anything else?"

Grozniak gave Agent Unger a wave of her hand, as though turning me over to his clutches, and he spoke for the first time. "Because of the tip, we arranged a lockdown and search of the jail. Guards recovered a burner cellphone in the common area of his unit. It was wiped clean—physically and electronically. We obtained a search warrant for its records and discovered the phone sent a single message."

Which meant they already knew it hadn't come to me. They had been on a fishing expedition. There's something more.

He pulled a piece of paper from his pocket, unfolded and read it, and handed it to me.

You know me by my Celtic Cross and Results Guaranteed.

Offer: $2.5 million for escape.

I'm patient.

My hands shook while I re-read the message. The Happy Reaper had told me he'd escape and when he did, he would kill my family, leaving me for last. I handed it back. "He has a Celtic cross tattoo on his lower back. The cross and 'Results Guaranteed' are also on his business card. But lots of people know that. Could another prisoner be setting him up? Send a text and leave the phone where guards could find it? Either way, he didn't send this to me. Who did it go to?"

"Another burner phone," Agent Grozniak said. "Your scenario is possible, but odds are it's him. Our problem,

Mr. McCree, is we don't know how many phones he's used. Whatever you and your family have going with Smith, you're in way over your head. Best you cooperate with us and put this behind you. What do you say?"

"I'm afraid I have nothing I can tell you." *Or at least nothing I* will *tell you.*

Knocking at the front door followed by the continuous buzz of the doorbell saved me from their next question. "There's a house showing," I said. "I need you to leave."

"You're making a big mistake, Mr. McCree," Agent Grozniak said. "We can protect you if we work together. Is your son here?"

"Sorry, no." I grabbed my crutches and yelled toward the entrance, "Coming." Speaking over my shoulder to the agents I added, "Shall I have him call you?"

Grozniak caught up to me. "Here's my card. Make sure he calls today. Let me get that for you."

With Agent Unger in tow, she opened the door. "We were just leaving." To me she said, "Consider our offer. We'll be in touch."

TWO

Despite my morning of interruptions, I was ready when Paddy picked me up, and we arrived at Kavanaugh's ten minutes early. Seated at a table, we awaited Colleen Carpetti.

"Relax, Dad," Paddy said. "What's the worst that can happen?"

Colleen had assisted my Uncle Mike when he set up semi-legal corporate entities to help families of deceased cops. The help was legal; where the money originated was not. With his death, I needed her expertise to close those corporations in a manner that didn't harm the families or expose the not-so-legal underpinnings of the charity. Paddy knew that, but Uncle Mike's philanthropy wasn't the worry causing my palms to sweat. Nor was my renewed concern about Happy Reaper issues. "If I knew, I wouldn't be nervous. I'd panic." I used my jeans to dry my hands and reached toward the second glass of water the waiter had poured for me. Stop, I told myself, or you'll spend the entire lunch hobbling to the restroom.

"That's ridiculous," Paddy said. "You offered to meet. She chose your favorite bar in Boston for lunch. You told me she sounded delighted that you had called. Worst case, you trade Uncle Mike stories."

Kavanaugh's was Uncle Mike's favorite Boston bar, not mine. His death was the reason I had met Colleen twenty-three days ago—not that anyone was counting. Paddy had a limited notion of what could be the worst thing to happen because he didn't know I wanted her to take a DNA test to determine if she was related to the McCrees. Prying into someone's life could lead to many unintended consequences, and dealing with family secrets—

"Holy shit, Dad. You didn't tell me she was gorgeous."

I followed Paddy's gaze to the front door. Colleen was allowing her eyes to adjust to the dim lighting. I waved my hand above my head until I captured her attention. "Remember, you're a married man."

"And," Paddy shot me a puzzled glance, "she looks like she could be my sister."

The only time I had met Colleen occurred in the hospital. I'd been on pain meds recovering from ankle surgery, and my memory was fuzzy. My recollection was she had McCree ice-blue eyes, and something about her face had reminded me of pictures of my mother when she was younger. "Uncanny, isn't it? No worries. She *is not* your sister." I suspected she was Paddy's cousin, that Uncle Mike had arranged for my sister, Ailish, to give up an illegitimate child by having one of his friends adopt the baby.

Colleen's gait was easy, confident. The long legs of her 5'10" frame ate up the path to our table against the rear wall. She wore tailored slacks, a short-sleeved blouse displaying toned muscles and a fading summer tan. The leather cross-body bag slung over her shoulder flashed neon colors as it swung with her steps.

She was thirty-two and she was gorgeous—not with the sharp angles of an anorexic-thin model, but with the glow of a woman who took the time with make-up to hide whatever flaws she might have accumulated and the confidence to let everyone gawk in her wake, which I noticed every male in the place was doing.

She offered her hand to Paddy, who had risen at her approach. "You must be Patrick. The beard is new, isn't it?"

Her eyebrows arched with her greeting, her eyes twinkling with interest—the same look Megan produced when she'd convinced me to read her a story. Colleen's smile was contagious. My face pulled into a wide grin.

"It's an experiment," Paddy replied. "My daughter likes it. My mother and grandmother don't, and my father may not have noticed."

"I noticed," I said. "It's not my mug. Why should I care?"

Paddy pulled out her chair. She thanked him and settled it back to the table herself. At Colleen's suggestion, because she was on a short leash from work, we ordered.

"You're looking much better than when I last saw you," Colleen said to me. "How's rehab going?"

"Slowly, but surely."

Paddy chuckled. "Dad wants to go three times as fast and work three times as hard as the PT thinks he should. It's driving him crazy. Which means he's driving us crazy."

"I'm not an ideal patient. I never realized how important being active is to my mental health. Reading's great, but after a while—"

"Suffice it to say, my father gets frustrated with having nothing he considers important to do."

"Enough about me," I said. "Thanks for taking time to meet us. I was a little surprised by a Monday lunch given what I guessed of your work schedule."

"Your timing was perfect." Her smile warmed her face. "My current audit client is a nonprofit in D.C. Unlike us, they celebrate Columbus Day. I have a rare Monday in the office and fly down tomorrow." She pulled a cellphone from her bag and laid it on the table. "I have to watch the time. The firm's managing partner realized I was in and scheduled a last-minute meeting. I'm sorry this will have to be so short. I should just dive in and ask my favor. If that's okay?"

I settled into my seat. *Maybe I won't have to ask her to take a DNA test; maybe she'll ask us.* "Sure," I said. "Shoot."

"A little background," she said. "Your Uncle Mike thought you walked on water, Seamus. I don't know how many times he told me the story about how you quit your job as the top-rated banking stock analyst because one of your bosses changed your report."

Crud. Not DNA. "That was a long time ago."

"Yes, but it's a lesson in standing up for what you believe in. Uncle Mike's rule number two."

"Wait," Paddy said. "Did he give you the same three rules as he gave my father?"

"Probably," she said. "One, honor my parents and three, never drink alone. I solved that one by not drinking." At my surprised look she added, "Empty calories, not religious principle."

"Same," I said. Seeing Paddy's confusion, I added, "Rules, not the no drinking."

She smiled. "And he was so proud you created the financial crimes unit for Criminal Investigations Group. He said you're a genius at following money trails."

Where was this going? "CIG is also ancient history."

"Here's where I have to take a risk and share something confidential. Given—"

The waiter interrupted us, delivering a beer for Paddy and sparkling water for Colleen. He assured us our lunches were coming soon and left. Colleen leaned in and lowered her voice.

"I'm up for partnership this year. As you know, it's a big fucking deal. With profit margins down, accounting firms are making fewer partners than they used to. I have a good chance, but . . ." She pressed her fingers to her brow. "This gives me such a headache. I think the senior partner for this client is hiding its fraud. If I suggest such a thing, it will totally kill my chance at partnership unless I'm one hundred percent correct and can prove it six ways from Sunday."

She sipped her water. She hadn't yet broken any confidences. We didn't know who the client was, or the partner, or any details. Would she cross the line?

"I want partnership." She wagged a finger in the air. "But not if the whole firm is crooked. I don't think it is. Until I understand how this scheme works, I can't be sure. When you contacted me to get together, it seemed like an answer to my prayers. You investigate financial crimes. Maybe you can figure it out, because—" She tapped her chest. "In my heart, I know there's a problem, and I won't let it go."

"Maybe," I said, "if I still had all CIG's resources at my disposal I could help, but they only work on cases upon police request. Anyway, I don't. If you couldn't follow a paper trail with all the information you have available for your audit, there's no way I can do better."

Colleen beamed her full smile on Paddy. "That's where you come in. Unless Uncle Mike was just bragging, I understand you have excellent computer skills. If I get you access to all the client's emails, you just—easy for me to say—just sift through them and maybe find a smoking gun?"

Paddy looked startled. "That's probably illegal."

"But if I give them to you as part of my auditing work? Give you written permission and provide my login info. Wouldn't that cover you?"

I stated the obvious. "You'd lose your job if they found out."

"Which is why Patrick can't get caught."

"Paddy doesn't hack anymore," I said. "Waiter's coming."

The waiter's arrival gave me time to evaluate the woman sitting opposite me. It took brass balls to ask Paddy to accept such a risk. Maybe she didn't understand it? I didn't sense an implied threat. As accountant to Uncle Mike's illegally funded charitable enterprises, she had enough dirt on us to get us in trouble. The reverse was also true. We could assure she'd lose her job.

Paddy and Colleen had ordered garden salads. I'd gone for a burger and steak fries. I cut the burger in half and checked the center. A perfect pink. "You a vegetarian like Paddy?"

"With all the travel I do, I need to watch my weight." She turned her smile on Paddy. "How long have you been vegetarian?"

"I kinda eased into it in junior high. What did you have in mind for me?"

She finished chewing and set her fork on her plate. "I can point your father to the suspicious payments and provide him with an internal paper trail. Of course, I'd love to see what the financial records on the other side of the transaction showed, but I don't have access. If I give you several email addresses, can you find correspondence to support—or I suppose refute—my supposition?"

The burger no longer had taste for me. I didn't want Paddy getting involved. He had used his illicit skills to cover my mother's tracks, and the police were suspicious about wonky phone records they had encountered investigating our capture of the Happy Reaper. The FBI planned to talk with Paddy. The smart part of me wanted to say no to Colleen and steer the conversation to comparing our DNA.

But I'm not one to ignore requests from damsels—or even guys— in distress, especially in dealing with uncovering financial crimes. I wanted to help, but I sure didn't want Paddy crossing any legal lines. "Why don't you walk me through the information that makes you suspect the senior partner, and I play devil's advocate? No risk to you." Her eyebrows scrunched together, so I continued my sales pitch. "Look, I know you're convinced, but a second set of eyes can't hurt, and maybe I can verify your suspicion without resorting to anything that gets anyone in trouble. Deal?" I shot Paddy a look I hoped he'd read as "Don't screw this up."

"Give me a moment to think," she said.

We finished our meals. Despite the lull in our conversation, Kavanaugh's had become louder, the place now filled with patrons. Colleen set her fork across her plate and reached into her bag, pulled out something I couldn't see, and held it in her lap. She leaned toward us. We followed her example. "Reach your hand under the table, Seamus. I have everything on a solid-state drive."

Kind of cloak and dagger. She placed the drive in my hand and wrapped my fingers around it.

"Don't get up," she said. "I'm flying back Friday afternoon. Can you finish by then?"

Paddy didn't let me answer. "Why don't you come by my mom's house in Cambridge on your way home from the airport?" Paddy said. "It's hardly out of your way and we can talk without having to shout. I'll cook. What's your favorite meal?"

She laid a hand on his arm. "Surprise me."

THREE

MEGAN, MY ONE-AND-SO-FAR-ONLY GRANDCHILD, met Paddy and me at the door upon our return from lunch with Colleen. "Grampa Seamus," she squealed in that three-year-old pitch that hurts adult ears. "You promised." She held out her newest favorite game, *Sequence for Kids.*

I loved spending time with Megan, although Lizzie wasn't sure if my influence was all positive. She'd given me a t-shirt, "Grampa. The Man. The Myth. The Bad Influence."

Keeping in mind to pick my spots to apply the bad influence part of my persona, I said, "Pumpkin, don't you have to take a nap?"

"Gema said I could play."

Lizzie, her "Gema," gave me a confirming nod.

"Is everyone playing?" I asked.

"Three games, Megan," Lizzie said, "then nap time. You and your father set up the board. Grampa Seamus and I will be right there."

Megan trotted off as if she were riding a magic horse, shoes slapping the wood floor. Paddy traded his shoes for slippers and followed.

Lizzie gave a dramatic sigh. "I'll need a nap when Megan takes hers. Keeping up with that child . . ." She held my crutches, allowing me to lean against the wall and change my footwear. "You know you don't have to remove your shoes."

"I can't help with the cleaning, so at least I can avoid bringing in dirt. It's been an interesting day." I summarized the FBI visit—Paddy had called and agreed on a time to meet them tomorrow—and our lunch with Colleen. "Paddy's convinced she's related. He thinks I knocked up some girl."

"Well, you weren't exactly a blushing virgin when we met."

"Yeah, but I did the math based on her birthday. I wasn't seeing anyone around the time she was conceived. And, I didn't have any flings." At Lizzie's skeptical look, I added. "I'll take all bets on this and bank the proceeds."

"I'll reserve judgment until I meet her on Friday," Lizzie said. "On a different note, I have good news and bad news."

She didn't give me a choice of the good or bad, which had been our married patter. "The buyer thought the FBI agents were competition and made a full-priced offer on the first-floor condo. The bad news is it's a cash deal closing in ten days."

"That's great news." I felt pleased on her behalf. "What's wrong with that?"

"You'll be homeless."

"That's good news, too. I love having Patrick and Megan here, but it's time for them to return to Chicago. This forces the issue. I'll book a room at an extended-stay hotel and hire whatever help I need."

"I was worried you'd object."

From the next room came Megan's call, "Gema, Grampa Seamus, come on."

"Coming," I yelled. "Let's play the games, get Megan to bed, and you, Paddy, and I can talk through how to transition. It's time I stood on my own one foot." *Not to mention that I want Paddy as far away from those FBI agents as possible.*

MEGAN WAS DRAGGING OUT OUR third game of *Sequence for Kids* to avoid her nap. A short-long-short buzz from the doorbell gave her a reprieve. She raced to the front door, her father in pursuit, reminding her not to answer the door for any strangers.

"You expecting visitors?" Lizzie asked me.

"I hope it's not the damned FBI again." Just saying their name conjured the smell of the guy's aftershave and I choked back a gag reflex.

Lizzie and I listened to Paddy tell Megan to move out of the way. He must have opened the well-oiled door because the next thing I heard was the rasp of the screen door opening, followed by Paddy's, "Are you okay?"

I guessed Megan must have taken a tumble and waited for a wail from her. After a beat, Paddy said, "No problem. We were finishing a game."

From the look on Lizzie's face, Paddy's half of the conversation didn't make sense to her either.

Megan raced in, announcing, "It's a lady." Patrick followed, ushering in Colleen. Pinched lips replaced the smile she had worn earlier. Furrows creased her brow.

"Mom," Paddy said, "this is Colleen Carpetti. Colleen, this is my mother, Elisabeth Lane, and my daughter, Megan." They exchanged handshakes and mumbled greetings.

"Can she play with us?" Colleen's arrival had wound her up. Getting her settled for a nap would be a challenge.

Colleen squatted to Megan's level and pointed to the game box. "It says only four players. Can you sit on my lap, and I'll watch while you finish your game? You can teach me how to play."

Megan squealed with delight.

GAME OVER, LIZZIE OFFERED MEGAN the chance to cut out cookies. Perhaps thinking she had avoided a nap, Megan gave Colleen a hug and accepted the deal.

"That was nice of you," I said.

"Great kid." Colleen released a long breath. "They fired me. I don't know how they found out, but they must have, because what they said is *so* bogus." Anger boiled off her like steam rising from a rainforest after a downpour.

"I'm sorry." I responded from habit. On this, I had no reason to feel guilty. "Maybe it would help to start from the beginning?"

"An HR person was with Gerry—Gerry Scigliano, the firm's managing partner, when I arrived for my meeting. Gerry fired me for sexual harassment. Can you believe it?" She pounded her thighs with closed fists. "The charge comes from the same client I told you about. HR and Legal found the guy and his written claim credible, and . . . and they escorted me from the building. I go back tonight to clear out my office. Under supervision."

Flinging her arms out as if she could throw away her anger, she said, "It is one hundred percent false. Never, never, never have I made an advance, said anything suggestive, told lewd jokes, or laughed at other people's.

Nothing. I'm lesbian. I'm not even attracted to guys. Yet there's not one damn thing I can do because they have this asshole's notarized statement."

Remains of the burger churned in my stomach. The room felt hot. *Easy, Seamus. Fire down.* She didn't need my anger to add to hers; she needed me to listen.

"Did he proposition you and you turned him down?" Paddy asked.

"If he did, I sure don't remember. He's lying, but it's a he-said-she-said deal, and the firm already decided. No, this is retaliation. It's got to be Hodkin—Hodkin Stuart, the senior partner involved with the suspect client. This removes me from the account and forces me out the door. If I can prove my suspicions . . ."

She didn't finish her thought, which made me wonder if her motivation had changed from doing the right thing to revenge. I believed her, but a little part of my brain reminded me that great liars are believable. Didn't matter. Endorphins beat logic. I was ready to take up the battle for truth, justice, and the Seamus McCree way: find the facts and let the chips fall as they may.

"Do they know you're lesbian?"

"I don't flaunt it, but I don't hide it, either. No way I'll mix my money with my honey. The sad truth is with the hours I work—used to work—I have no time for a relationship."

"Tell them," Paddy said. "Threaten to sue for wrongful termination. Get your job back."

Paddy had been an entrepreneur and an independent consultant. He hadn't spent time in corporate settings and didn't understand the damage already done. Colleen could sue, but even if she regained her job with back pay and damages, the firm would respond with crap assignments, give her the worst performers for her team. Plus, if the fraud she suspected was widespread, she wouldn't want to work there.

"Did they accuse you of downloading the documents you gave me?"

She shook her head. "It's just too big a coincidence."

Paddy asked, "Have you mentioned your concerns to anyone at work?"

"Only to Hodkin, the partner in charge of the account. Preliminary audit notes include everything we have to reconcile before releasing our report, so I listed the possible fraud. Hodkin told me they had looked at the issue an earlier year, and it was not a concern. I complied with his request to remove it from the items to reconcile."

She worried her water glass in a tight circle. "I suppose someone could have seen them before I removed them. Last week, I downloaded the data and typed the covering memo to help you understand the issues. You're thinking I tipped off someone that I remained concerned?"

Paddy asked to see the memo. We booted a laptop, attached the external drive Colleen had given me, and read the memo together. Paddy leaned back, staring at the ceiling. "You created this at work?"

She had.

Paddy tapped the word "fraud" on the screen. "I'll bet," he said, "they have sniffer software. Lots of companies use it for email and other material. It's like what email programs use to decide whether something is spam. It looks for keywords and sends an alert whenever it finds them. An accounting firm might want a heads-up with a word like fraud or a phrase like," he tapped the screen again, "suspicious payments."

"They can do that?" Colleen beat me to asking.

"Perfectly legal," Paddy said. "And easy with centralized computing."

"So, I screwed myself."

"Maybe," Paddy said. "Depending on their software, they could discover what you downloaded. Since they didn't accuse you of that, maybe they don't know. Either way, we'd better secure this stuff somewhere they can't find it."

"Assuming with what you now know, Colleen," I said, "you still want to pursue this?"

Her eyes grew wide. "Because if I do, you think they'll smear my name with this allegation?"

Our silence answered her question.

"Being let go is a huge black mark. I won't let that stop me from finding the truth. Are you willing to help?"

"They've scored the first goal," I said. "To even things we need to press our attack. To win, we keep maximum pressure on."

Paddy shook his head. "Dad just subjected you to the Seamus McCree soccer analogy number three. It means yes, and we'd better get cracking."

"Tell me about this Hodkin Stuart guy," I said.

"His mother is the sister of the Howes of the firm, Franklin, Howe and Howe. He's an Ivy Leaguer—Brown, I think. Worked two years at one of the big four accounting firms before switching to FHH. A little snooty, but nice enough."

Did he rise to partner because he deserved it or because he was a Howe? That question showed my suspicion born of working-class roots and experience with the old-boy network during my employment on Wall Street. "Is he good at his job?"

"He keeps his clients happy. His technical skills are rusty, but that's why they have us."

"But he'd know fraud if he tripped over it?" I asked.

"Oh, sure. You're never too rusty for that."

"Meaning," I said. "either it's not a problem, or he's covering it up."

Lizzie came into the room. "Megan's napping. Are we going to have time to talk?"

Colleen looked embarrassed and stood.

I also rose, leaning on the chair. "I'll look at the material tonight. Can we meet here tomorrow, say ten?"

FOUR

WITH MEGAN DOWN FOR HER nap, we had forty-five minutes tops to sort through a gazillion issues facing us. Paddy and Lizzie sat opposite me. I propped my throbbing left ankle on the fourth chair.

"Patrick," Lizzie said. "I don't want you to stay here in Cambridge. You're too convenient for the FBI. Besides, it's been three weeks and Megan needs to get back with her mother."

Paddy manufactured a raft of objections. He had play dates planned for Megan. I still needed him to assist in my care wherever I stayed. He could more easily help Colleen if he was local and they could review together whatever he discovered. Lizzie countered each one, including stealing my line about me needing to stand on my own one foot.

Neither was backing down, and I wondered if Paddy's intransigence was because he worried about my mental state.

"Paddy," I said. "Are you concerned I'm depressed? I'm committed to my rehab. Feeling antsy about my limited mobility is a good sign. If I were depressed, being trapped inside wouldn't bother me. It will weigh more on me if I don't start working toward independence. I hate being selfish, but I will be. Honestly, it's better for me if you leave."

He shook his head and rolled his eyes. Three quick buzzes from the front door preempted his objection.

"The agent's supposed to bring me the contract to sign," Lizzie said. "I'll just be a moment. Hold your thought, Patrick."

I knew Paddy was steaming and my gambit hadn't worked. I shifted my ankle and couldn't hide my grimace. Not helping my cause. To avoid his thundercloud expression, I stared at my good foot.

Multiple footsteps headed toward us.

"Patrick McCree," Agent Grozniak said, "I know we're scheduled to meet tomorrow morning, but we'd like you to participate in a lineup. We have a witness who says you hauled two suitcases through Mr. Smith's Airbnb parking lot."

Paddy did not accept the FBI's offer, stating he needed to have counsel present before he took part in any lineups. He had no defense counsel because until their arrival, he'd had no reason to need one. They tried the if-you're-innocent-you-have-nothing-to-fear-guilt-trip crap.

Lizzie went into mother-grizzly mode. "You see yesterday's paper? They had a story on a guy imprisoned for twenty-eight years for a murder he didn't commit. Once you people get your teeth on a suspect, you manufacture your case to fit your beliefs."

She ordered them out of her house and to stay away unless they had a warrant.

Paddy restrained his mother. "It's okay, Mom, they're just doing their job." To the agents, he added, "We'll meet as agreed tomorrow unless my attorney counsels against that."

"I thought," Agent Unger said, "you didn't have an attorney."

"I will tomorrow," Paddy said. "Let me show you out."

They left, which meant they didn't yet have enough evidence to arrest Paddy. Yet. He and Lizzie went upstairs to work on securing him legal counsel. If I could convince the Happy Reaper to recant his story of my mother hiring him, it would remove motivation for Paddy's "supposed" actions.

Unlikely? Maybe. But it's all I had.

A phone call informed me that visiting hours for the Happy Reaper's prison section weren't until Thursday afternoon. Three days seemed like forever, so I called Chief Riley of Leominster. He knew my mom through his friendship with Uncle Mike, who had retired from the Boston Police Department with the rank of captain. The necessary chit chat revolved around my mother. I assured Riley that she was recovering well from her heart attack and segued to asking if he could get me in to see the Happy Reaper other than during normal visiting hours.

In the following silence, I pictured him scratching his head. "You know," he said, "it's the county sheriff who runs the jail."

"The problem is, if the Happy Reaper keeps to his bogus story, all kinds of other things may come into play. Things I thought you agreed wouldn't be in anyone's interest." I was tap dancing because, in the past, Riley had been vague regarding how much he knew about Uncle Mike's charitable undertakings.

"And you think visiting him will change that?"

Sounding more confident than I was, I said, "I do."

"I'll see what I can do and get back to you."

It was the best I could hope for. To avoid thinking about the Happy Reaper, I retrieved Colleen's drive and plugged it into my computer.

FIVE

TUESDAY MORNING BROUGHT A CRISP autumn day to Cambridge. I opened the windows to air my rooms, bundled up against the chill, and sat on the front stoop, waiting for Colleen to arrive. My cellphone rang—a minor miracle that I remembered to have it with me. The display said Colleen.

"Someone is following me," she said

My first thought was wondering if the FBI knew of her role in Uncle Mike's charities. *Stay calm, Seamus.* "I've had that happen to me," I said. "I assume you don't know who it is?"

"A gray sedan. Mercedes, maybe? Mass. plates. For sure a guy. If I'm right, I don't want to lead him to you. What do you think?"

She might be paranoid, but best to be prudent. "Drive to one of the big hospitals. Doesn't matter which one. Park in a lot and walk in the main entrance. You'll see if anyone follows you. If they do, find a police officer. Assuming they don't, follow signs for lab work or radiology, whatever. Then slip out a side entrance. Walk a few blocks and catch a ride to the Boudreau Branch of the Cambridge Library." I gave her the address.

"It's near here," I said. "I'll get Paddy to drop me off before—" No reason Colleen had to know Paddy needed to meet with a defense attorney that morning. "Don't worry how long it takes. I have no problem entertaining myself in a place filled with books."

By the time we hung up, she sounded relieved. Not me. My heart was pounding in my chest like it was trying to get out.

The Boudreau branch was less than a mile from Lizzie's house. Paddy and Megan had gone to the tiny library several times for story hour. Lizzie had borrowed a series of books that we took turns reading with Megan. I had never been there, so it surprised me when Paddy stopped the car in front of what looked like a storefront.

"Good luck with the defense attorney," I said.

"It's not him I'm worried about," Paddy said, "It's the witness. I crossed paths with a leggy blond in the parking lot. I don't think she got a good look at me. Plus, I was clean-shaven and wearing a hat."

So that's why he grew a beard. I waved him off. "Let me know if there's anything I can do."

A circular green sign proclaimed the Alma Boudreau Observatory Hill Branch of the Cambridge Public Library. I crutched myself inside and found two chairs flanking a small circular end table. I plopped onto one chair and rested my crutches against the other and pulled out the pages I had printed out from the disk Colleen had given me.

She walked through the door shortly before eleven. She wore a short denim jacket over a teal t-shirt, her leather bag slung over her shoulder. Jeans, no belt, and trainers completed her outfit. She'd pulled her hair into a ponytail that bounced with each powerful step. Walking around the checkout desk, she presented her profile. My stomach knotted at an indistinct memory—not a good one. Who did she resemble, and what was the bad memory?

Looking at her straight on, the feeling dissipated. I brushed the vibe away and made her welcome by removing the crutches from the second chair. "Did they follow you into the hospital?"

"Don't think so." Still standing, she pointed to the paperwork on the table. "What do you think?"

I motioned her to the seat and, following her lead, stifled my normal tendency to ask how she was. "I didn't have time to review everything on your disk, but I could follow your trail, and I share your concern." She looked nervously over her shoulder. "We can watch the door from here."

She placed her chair to half face me and the front door and sat. I continued. "What you have are three unusual circumstances. In combination, they look suspicious. Each anonymous donation to Harpoon Services comprised historical documents supposedly worth more than fifty thousand dollars. They've never accepted historical material. Instead of selling them to support their programs, they donated them to the historical societies. They acted as an intermediary. Correct?"

"Exactly. And days before the first donation, Harpoon instituted a new policy to prevent the director from knowing anonymous donors' names. Now it's only the Grants Administrator and Board Chairman."

"Conveniently, your accuser and his father. What do you know about them?"

"Chambers Austin, Jr., the father, is a force. The Austins made their first money in whaling, then switched to textiles. They were fading until Junior created a venture capital firm headquartered in Newburyport. It made a fortune during the computer boom of the seventies and eighties. He founded Harpoon Services and is still the chairman."

"Aha, the Harpoon moniker relates to his family's whaling. Interesting. And his son?"

She gritted her teeth and pushed on the arms of the chair. "Far as I can see, he's a small chip off his father's block. Chambers Austin III likes to be called Aussie. I don't know much about him. Late twenties."

From Paddy's research I knew he was twenty-seven. He'd bounced around boarding schools and took six years to graduate from a second-tier university. Daddy created the Grants Administrator position at Harpoon to give Aussie a job.

"Anyway," she continued, "those transactions had a whiff of tax fraud, and I put them on the exception list to verify."

"Because you think they inflated appraisals to justify a bigger tax deduction? But the charity doesn't determine the appraisal. That's the donor's responsibility."

"True." She blew out a long breath. "But why be the intermediary and, if there is fraud, become a party to it? I presented this to Hodkin Stuart, the audit partner-in-charge. He told me it was at the request of a large donor. He said they had done something similar a few years ago. I accepted that until I learned that my accounting contact at Harpoon, who's been there a decade, had no recollection of any such thing. Plus, in the last five years, the largest anonymous donation was only ten grand."

"It didn't meet your smell test."

"I was prepared to let it go until my Harpoon contact

told me it had just happened again. Making it once a quarter for four quarters. I called several of the historical societies—I forget where, Podunk, Indiana, Bumfuck, Ohio, tiny places. That's when I thought of you, and you know the rest."

A mother pushing a stroller and with three kids under the age of five in tow entered the library, changing it from a place of hushed conversation to kids' loud whispers, making it difficult for me to concentrate. We waited until they moved to the children's section before continuing our discussion.

"What," I said, "did you hope I could do?"

"Before they shit-canned me, I wanted you to determine whether I was right or wrong. *Now*, I want to take the bastards down."

I wasn't sure which bastards she was referring to, but that could wait. "And if you're wrong?"

A wry smile crept onto her face. "I no longer consider that a possibility, but I wonder if I'm paranoid. Why would someone follow me?"

"You haven't had strange phone calls? People hanging up? No stalkers?" She shook her head no. "Did anyone know of your work for Uncle Mike? Did he ever introduce you to anyone else involved?"

The surprise on her face told me she hadn't considered that possibility. "Uncle Mike's nosy neighbor lady saw me going to his apartment, but she doesn't know anything of his philanthropic pursuits. Assuming I wasn't imagining being followed, it must relate to this." She waved at the papers between us. "Someone wants to know what I'm doing. Why?"

"In today's environment, they'd have to worry you'll

sue them. What happened when you went to retrieve your personal effects at the office?"

"A woman from HR accompanied me and checked to make sure I didn't take any company property or files. Made a list of all the files I left in drawers. I got a copy. Gave me a receipt for my computer and key. Shooed away a co-worker who probably wondered what happened. I'm sure I'm the big water-cooler topic. Kind of surprising no one has called me."

"They might not want to do it from work. But the point is, you didn't get the feeling anyone followed you last night?"

She shook her head. "Just this morning and now I'm doubting that."

"Trust your instincts. We'll plan some counter-surveillance and see if we can trap them. Tell me about your accuser."

"To be honest, I never directly worked with him. It's not a large office, so he was frequently around, but my dealings were with the director and the guy in finance. I thought I got along with them fine. Aussie—Austin Chambers the Third—is a frat-boy-salesman type. You know, a wise-cracking, back-slapping, whitened-teeth kind of guy."

"So even if you were into guys, not your type. He ever hit on you?"

She grimaced. "Never copped a feel, if that's what you mean."

"Ask you to dinner? Lunch?" My phone chirped a message. From Chief Riley, it said. "Visit w/ Happy R this afternoon. Be at the police station by 1:00."

I couldn't drive. Paddy wasn't available. Lizzie was

working. I needed a taxi or one of those ride shares Paddy was extolling that I had never used. And I had to decide now.

"Seamus?"

I snapped out of my mental frazzle. "Sorry. I have to leave now."

"What?" Her voice rose in disbelief. The librarian glared, "SILENCE!" at us.

"I still want to help, but this is urgent." I gave her a quick explanation of where I was going, but not why, other than that my family was in trouble. As I was promising to call her to make plans, she was pressing buttons on the phone. Probably texting a friend about what an asshole I was.

"He'll be here in three minutes," she said. At my bewildered expression she held out her phone. "My Lyft app. We can talk on the ride to Leominster."

SIX

THE LYFT DRIVER'S CONSTANT PATTER made it impossible for us to talk, and our lack of response wasn't slowing him. "I'm sorry," I said. "We need to chat. Maybe you should turn on your favorite radio station."

Rap doesn't do anything for me, but it provided cover noise to give us privacy.

"I've been trying to remember my interactions with Aussie," Colleen said. "He never hit on me, but maybe he invited me to dinner. You think he invented the harassment claim because I blew him off and didn't fall for his charms?"

"I don't believe in coincidences. More like he's a tool for someone, like his daddy. Let's attack this thing on several fronts and give your former employer a few things to think about." I ticked the items on my fingers.

"One, if you think someone is following you again, drive to the Department of Labor office. Make an appointment to talk to someone about a sex-discrimination issue."

"But this had nothing to do with me being female."

"How many female partners do they have? Zero, right? It may not have anything to do with you being a woman, but nobody wants the DOL sniffing around their firm. This gets them worrying about their business."

Her raised eyebrows suggested she thought I was crazy.

"The person following you will tell your bosses.

They're smart fellas. They'll figure out why you went to the DOL."

"You want me to lead them on a wild goose chase?"

"They'll worry that you'll sue them. Even if they believe they'll win, a suit still costs money and time. Let's feed their concerns. Two," I raised a second finger, "talk to your work friends this evening. Find out what they were told. Hint you're planning to fight it. Tell them you've contacted a top-notch employment lawyer—we'll have you do that, but first we have to determine who's good, and we can't do that reading billboards along the highway."

"I don't have that kind of money."

"They work on contingency." *Unlike Paddy's defense attorney. Be here, Seamus. Be now.* "If they're interested in your case, you don't have any up-front cost. If you talk to enough people at the company, one of them will snitch to the bosses."

"That's a jaded view of the world."

"We show them our right hand: you counter-punching against your dismissal. They'll spend time and energy figuring out what you're up to. Meanwhile, the left hand looks at the accounting fraud."

"How?"

The sixty-four-thousand-dollar question. "The key is determining who the anonymous donor is. For that, I need your help."

"You have a plan?" Her mouth crooked with skepticism.

"Elbow grease. Phone calls and computer sleuthing." I presented the bones of my idea.

"That's the best we have?"

"When a museum accepts historical documents," I said, "they want to know they're real, not fake. They require provenance as part of the authentication process. Right?"

"Yes, but, Seamus," Colleen said in the same tone Paddy used to explain a difficult concept to Megan, "we're not talking the Smithsonian here. These are small museums and the donations came from a Washington, D.C. charity. They'll assume the charity or the appraiser checked things out."

"But where did the stuff originally come from? Is there a collective theme tying them together? If we find that, maybe we can finger the donor."

"I can call the museums," Colleen said, "but why would they talk to me?"

"Tell them the truth. You're an accountant trying to verify donations before you sign off on financial statements. Routine, but you desperately need their help. Reach a few people with helper-personalities, and they'll bend over backwards for you."

"Seamus, I'm not rich like you. If they add impersonation or whatever to the charges I might face on this sexual harassment crap . . . I need to keep my license."

She was right. I was lucky to have earned enough money and invested well enough to not have financial worries. "Can you toe the line, but not cross over? Let them draw the wrong conclusion. You *are* an accountant. You *are* trying to verify donations. The person probably knows you'd have to do that before you can approve the financial statements. Let them come to their own conclusions but record your phone calls."

"Can't. To legally record phone conversations in Massachusetts requires two-party-consent."

That might not have bothered me, but it did her. I rubbed my head to stimulate thoughts. My hands and scalp warmed up, but I'm not sure it did anything for my brain. "Write an exact script and follow it so you can show you never made false statements."

She considered my suggestion for a few miles. "It's my butt on the line if they bring me to a hearing, but if I do nothing I lose. You, at least, suggested something tangible I can do. But even if I get a list of the donated items, the charity, Harpoon Services, still acts as a shield to the donor. That's where we need to probe, and I can't talk with them. If they're crooked, they won't talk to anyone."

"We'll need the documents to lead us to a clue. If they were bought and sold, we should be able to determine those parties."

"Check eBay," she said.

"Plus, maybe a few of the museums will ask Harpoon questions, and the heat flows uphill."

For the rest of the trip Colleen went through her notes and made a list of museums to contact. I spent the time stressing out about meeting with the Happy Reaper.

OUR ROUTE TOOK US PAST the storage facility where I had shot and captured the Happy Reaper. I hadn't been this way since the incident. To my surprise, no feelings popped to the surface during our drive-by.

At the edge of Leominster, I dialed Chief Riley to tell him I was almost there. The Lyft driver pulled on to

Church Street and I released a long sigh. We passed the First Baptist Church and a firehouse, both constructed of older red bricks, and stopped in front of the police station, a mid-century modern creation of glass front, concrete, and lighter-colored bricks—something of a disappointment. "Wish me luck," I said.

"I'll hang at the library." Colleen held up her phone with a map outlining her route. "It's only a five-minute walk. Call when you're done. I hope you get what you want."

Colleen hopped out, hustled around the car to retrieve my crutches from the front seat, and handed them to me. By the time I was on the sidewalk, Chief Riley was walking toward us. "Stay right there, Seamus," he said. "I'll pull a car around. She can't come. It's—" He stopped mid-stride. "Have we met?"

"Colleen Carpetti." She offered a handshake. "At the hospital. We were both waiting to see Seamus."

"Right." Riley snapped his fingers. "Let's talk about that after I take Seamus to prison."

A tremor of concern rippled up my spine. He could have phrased that better. And what did he want to talk to Colleen about?

SEVEN

MY CRUTCHES WERE A PROBLEM at the prison. A potential weapon, they would not let me in with them. I couldn't walk without them. Chief Riley prevailed on them to get a wheelchair from the infirmary. A guard led us to an interview room deep inside the maximum-security wing of the jail. The room reeked of Pine-Sol and fear.

The Happy Reaper sat in a wheelchair parked at the table. Interconnected chains locked his arms, legs, and the wheelchair to an O-ring bolted into the floor.

"Seamus," his gesture toward my wheelchair rattled his chains, "trying for empathy? It's so good of you to visit. I'd offer you a pop, but I'm afraid the guards make lousy waitresses. Chief Riley, what a pleasure to see you again."

Following our plan, Riley signaled the guard and excused himself. "I've got a case of the runs," he said in explanation.

It was my first opportunity to look at the Happy Reaper up close. His face showed recent weight loss. He maintained his brown hair in a military haircut. In the prison's glaring lights, his eyes looked pale gray. Muscles corded his neck, and I surmised he was staying fit despite the gunshot wounds that kept him wheelchair bound.

"Recovering from your injuries?" I asked.

"Thanks for coming all this way to ask. The worst was not being able to sit. That's no longer a problem. Your mother doing well? I keep wondering where she got the money for the down payment."

A thousand questions raised their voices in my head. Focus on why you're here: determine what he requires in trade for the promise I want to extract from him.

"Your name is really John Smith?"

"True enough. Never found my Pocahontas and never made it to the Olympics—sprinting or wrestling—like my namesakes. But I did climb to the top of my chosen profession."

I left his ego unbruised. "The FBI visited me yesterday. They thought you were texting me from jail."

He swiveled his head and pointedly stared at the camera placed in the corner near the ceiling. "My telepathy must be strong, 'cause here you are. How's your mom doing? She was a pain-in-the-ass client, but she sure knows how to take charge. And your son? Granddaughter? Megan, isn't that her name? They wouldn't let me put a youngster on my visitor list."

Inside, I boiled at the implied threats. Outside, I plastered on a smile. "We've always been honest with each other, have we not?"

He canted his head as though giving the idea consideration. "We have. I figure you for a straight-shooter, although you were damned lucky to take me down before that gun ran out of bullets." He laughed at his joke.

I nodded appreciation for his wit and edged toward my pitch. "Yes, and you threatened that if I didn't let you go, you'd escape and kill everyone close to me before killing me."

"Come on, Seamus, this room has ears and eyes."

And I have five supporting witnesses. "Understood," I said. "Your threats against my family and friends are beneath you. As I understand it, you've always been careful to avoid collateral damage in your, uh, assignments. Everyone else at the storage unit that day would have let you go. Your beef is with me. This should be just between us. You were angry at being captured and made the threat because it might have allowed you to escape." I wiped the smile from my face. "I could be preemptive and contact the Irish mob and put a contract on you, but—"

Through a smirk he said, "Like mother like son."

I'd practiced my pitch in my head. Now I tried it on him. "But that's not how we do things, you and I. We deal directly with our issues. I shot you. I thwarted your schemes. You're here because of me, no one else. You've said it yourself, we're a lot alike—even though you kill people. We're both straight shooters."

A bad choice of words, but he *was* nodding, which I took as a good sign.

"Unlike some competitors, you—"

"I have no competitors. Only wannabes."

I needed him agreeing with me, not disagreeing about irrelevant logic. "Point taken. What I'm trying to say is that you make agreements and keep them. Maybe you get a thrill from killing, I don't know. But you're not a sicko serial killer. You're hired for a job and you honor your contract. If you get out of prison, it should be just the two of us. You attempt to eliminate me, and I try to throw you back in prison. Just us. *Mano a mano.*"

He clapped his hands together, chains rattling an offbeat accompaniment. "Bravo! Great speech. *Mano a mano* and leave out your family and friends. But you've missed two major points. First, in this hypothetical situation, I am my own client, right? Employer and employee. If my client specifies the order of extinguishing your lives, my 'Results Guaranteed' ethic requires the employee to follow the employer's wishes. Anything less diminishes the product's value. Don't you see?"

I saw. "But, as an employer, aren't you allowed to change your mind, make a different contract?"

"Sure," he lengthened the word, dripping it in sarcasm. "But why would I? I'm having a blast watching you suffer. It's written all over your face, worry lines carving your forehead. The very fact that you're gracing me with your presence. I'll admit, I thought your mother would come first. It's better that it's you. We wouldn't want her to say something incriminating while the video rolls." He shifted his head toward the camera.

He was goading me. To do what? Strike him? Threaten him? He'd pointed out the prison was taping the room, but he had sort of admitted to threatening me. Given the various death penalties he faced for multiple murders, no prosecutor would waste time and resources on a simple threat. Me threatening him was another matter.

I locked my fingers behind my head, leaning back to project a nonchalance as far from the burning in my gut as night is from day. I'd try goading him. "You surprise me, Mr. Smith—John Smith—how did it feel growing up with that handle? I didn't expect your pettiness and passion of the moment to be still coloring your judgment. It should be—"

"But it isn't, and you need to accept that, Seamus. I had two points, and you interrupted me from imparting my second piece of jail-house wisdom. To get something you must give something. You have nothing to offer me except entertainment. Every day and every night you'll wonder what I'm planning. You'll worry, have sleepless nights, get stress headaches." A smile lit his face. "I love picturing your distress. Until you find something better— much better—I have no motivation to change. You understand what I'm saying?"

Coming here had been a terrible mistake, another example of Seamus McCree hubris, thinking I could convince him. All I had done was to provide him with more pleasant memories to entertain him in his cell.

CHIEF RILEY AND I DIDN'T speak until we were in his car driving to his headquarters. "That was your big idea, come with your hat in hand to a guy who's killed hundreds of people? He owns that hat now. What an egotistical prick."

"You're right," I said. "I thought I could change his mind."

"I meant he was the egotistical prick. Although if the shoe fits . . ." He gave me time to take the bait. I kept my mouth shut, and he continued. "You should have killed him when you had the chance." He barked a laugh. "Not that I'm advocating it, but it sure would simplify things. It'll take forever for some state to stick a needle in his arm, and, in the meantime, he's spending his time working on a memoir."

Hearing him say aloud that I should have murdered the Happy Reaper was a surprise. It was a practical comment, but not a moral one. I texted Colleen that we were headed back and received an immediate reply: she'd meet me there and had already arranged transportation home. My text to Paddy asking how his meetings with the defense attorney and the FBI had gone received no response. Relax, I told myself; there was nothing I could do. My stiff neck and the beginnings of a tension headache suggested I needed to find better solutions than telling myself to relax.

Riley waited until I finished texting before starting his interrogation. "What's the scoop with Colleen Carpetti? Seeing you two together, she sure looks like she could be your daughter?"

"She's Bruno Carpetti's daughter. Uncle Mike never mentioned her?"

"Why would he? Mike was your dad's best friend and always there for your mother after your father died, but not a blood relative. Bruno Carpetti—worked in Boston with your dad and Mike before he became a state cop, right? She doesn't look a thing like him. Your mom meet her?"

Not yet, I thought, but maybe she should. What would happen if I sprung her on Mom? "She's adopted." I pointed to Colleen standing by a taxi. "There she is."

"Good. I can't wait to hear how she became friends with your Uncle Mike."

Good cops know if you're hiding something and Chief Riley was a good cop. How could I avoid subjecting Colleen to his friendly third degree? We pulled up behind the cab and Colleen ran to the car and opened the back door to grab my crutches,

"Perfect timing," she said. "The cab's ready to bring us to the station. If we hurry, we can catch the next train."

"Sorry, Chief," I said with relief, "we'll need a rain check."

"Say hello to your mom for me. I still want to hear about all of this." The sweep of his arm included Colleen.

Eight

THE FIRST THING I DID once the cab pulled away from the curb was call Paddy's cellphone. He didn't answer, and I considered calling Lizzie but rejected that idea. If she knew nothing about Paddy, my call would only upset her. Paddy would call me when he could.

At our approach to the train station, my mood brightened. I've enjoyed trains since I was a tadpole and felt pleased Colleen had discovered the Fitchburg line would take us to Boston's North Station. Growing up, the T provided cheap transport from South Boston. During my Wall Street days, I'd commuted into New York City by rail and preferred it for business trips up to Boston or down to D.C. Swaying trains and the clickity-clack of unwelded rail soothed me. I never tired of hearing the whistled Morse Code Q warning at road crossings.

I gave Colleen the window seat so the scenery wouldn't distract me and asked how the library had been.

"Didn't go. I found a quiet area in the city offices across the street from the police station, which was better since I didn't have to worry about talking. Volunteers staffed most of the museums I called. They either had no access to the information, were unwilling to talk about donations over the phone, or wanted the director or a board member to call me back. But the ones who did talk gave me all kinds of info."

She showed me several pages of notes and a summarized list, neat as a ledger sheet.

"Any themes crop up?"

"Several paintings of local scenes. Lots of Civil War correspondence, letters where the author mentioned the town or village he'd traveled through or fought near. And hometown boys. That sort of thing."

I scanned the detailed list. "Look," I pointed to two items. "Don't these sound like the same thing?"

Both letters were from a sergeant in the First Nebraska Volunteer Infantry to his parents. Dated January 13, 1863, he described a skirmish with guerrillas roaming the countryside in Arkansas. A museum in Nebraska near the parents' home received one letter; the second found its way to a small museum in the Ozarks near where the action took place.

"I was so busy getting the details, I missed that. I wonder if one's a copy."

"Or forgery," I said. "Do you think you can convince these two museums to join you on a conference call and have one read their letter while the other compares it to what they have?"

She flipped pages in her notes. "Neither mentions it's a copy. A thousand bucks for the one in Nebraska and twelve-fifty for Arkansas'. Any others like this?"

"Not on your list, but remember, you've only talked with four museums. If this is a pattern, you'll blow the lid off this thing."

"Thank you, thank you. I never saw the forest for all the weeds I was crawling through."

I smiled at the mixed metaphor. "You done good, but let's not jump to conclusions until we confirm our suspicion. Do you mind if we stop at my mother's on the way to pick up your car? She doesn't live far from North

Station. I'd like to check and confirm she's following the doctor's orders after her heart attack and triple bypass." *And I want to know how she reacts to seeing you.*

"No problem. Do you need to call her and make sure she's in?"

"With Mom, surprise often works best."

MOM WAITED AT THE OPEN door to her apartment watching me crutch off the elevator with Colleen. "Your color's looking good," I said. "How are you feeling?"

"Like I'm old."

I laughed. "Mom, you *are* old."

"Seamus," Colleen said from behind me, "that's no way to talk to your mother."

"I'm the only one who tells her the truth. She scares everyone else. Mom, let me introduce Colleen Carpetti. She helped Uncle Mike with the accounting aspects of his charity work."

Mom's mouth curved into a smile to welcome Colleen. Her eyes grew wide in what I took as surprise. A master at hiding her emotions, if I hadn't been watching, I would have missed the tell.

"I can see," Mom said, "why Mike O'Malley would want to keep someone so beautiful to himself. Won't you come in? Maybe I won't have to undergo my son's third degree with you here. I was just finishing up my daily darts practice. It's time for my cocktail. Can I get you something?"

Colleen looked to me for guidance, and I said, "Are you supposed to be drinking?"

"I'm going on eighty. If a drink a day kills me, so be it."

"Mom, you used to lie about your age and make yourself younger. You just turned seventy-nine a week ago. Are you now exaggerating how old you are?"

"Mr. Smarty Pants, I *am* going on eighty." She smacked my shoulder.

"We'll stay for one drink so I can give you the third degree. You been doing your exercises?"

"What will you have, Colleen?"

"A non-alcoholic beer? Sparkling water?"

"Seltzer?" Mom turned to me. "And you?"

"Can't drink because of the pain meds. I'll get tap water."

Mom led us to her kitchen, redolent from the beef and barley stew simmering on the stove. She fixed herself an Old Fashioned and poured Colleen's fizzy water into a tumbler. I shrugged off my knapsack and laid it on a kitchen chair hidden by the tablecloth and filled a mug with tap water.

Offering the glass to Colleen, Mom asked, "Is my son behaving himself?"

"He's been very helpful."

"You might have known Colleen's father," I said to gauge her reaction. "Bruno Carpetti?"

Mom smiled at the name, but the liquid in her glass magnified a hand-tremor I had never seen her have. She motioned us into the living room. The nineteen slice of the dart board held three darts.

"Mom, do you need to finish your practice? Looks like you've still got the rest of nineteen, and all the twenty slice and bullseyes to go for your 'round the world practice.'"

"Since my recent difficulties, I'm not as pedantic about finishing the exercise." Gesturing Colleen to the couch she added, "I used to be halfway decent at darts. You play?"

"Don't let her con you, Colleen. Mom's a ranked player and ambidextrous. She likes to offer to play with her right hand tied behind her back."

Mom put on an exaggerated look of disappointment. "Spoilsport. Bruno Carpetti. I haven't heard his name for years. How is he?"

Mom expressed her regret at his passing before interrogating Colleen in the guise of pleasant conversation. I sipped water and threw in a question here and there concerning Mom's health, next appointment, exercise—all the things she would expect me to ask. When they had both finished their beverages, I collected their glasses, holding them at the bottom to avoid mixing my DNA with their saliva on the rim. Refusing Colleen's offer of help, I crutched to the kitchen to wash them. Or so I told Mom. With the sound of hot water masking my actions, I found two zip-locked freezer bags. I put one glass in each bag and stored the bags in my backpack. I returned for my mug, washed it, and put it away.

In case Paddy had his ringer silenced, I tried texting him. No reply. Next stop, pick up Colleen's car and home to Lizzie's for, I hoped, news about Paddy. "'Bout ready to go, Colleen?" I called from the kitchen.

At her positive response, I shrugged on the knapsack. We made our goodbyes, and I escaped with my loot.

* * *

WE TOOK A CAB TO retrieve Colleen's car in the Beth Israel parking lot, where she had left it when she thought someone was following her. She dropped me at Lizzie's shortly before five o'clock. "Is nine too early tomorrow?" she asked.

"Wednesday my physical therapist tortures me for an hour starting at eight-thirty. Better make it ten. Thanks for schlepping me around all day."

"Thank *you* for helping me nail these bastards. I like your mother. She's a hoot."

I stifled the impulse to tell Colleen that Mom had been on her best behavior. If I was right and Colleen was a McCree, she'd have plenty of opportunity to see Mom in action. I crutched up the walk while Colleen left for an evening of talking with work associates and planting seeds.

I let myself in to a deserted first floor, my footsteps echoing the same way ideas were rattling around inside my head. In my knapsack I had DNA samples from Mom and Colleen. I didn't have a full understanding of how DNA testing worked, but by adding mine to the grouping, I was sure a lab had the necessary data to ascertain if Colleen was my half-sister, my niece, or not related.

Rather than rely on the Internet to find the "best" lab, I called the head of Criminal Investigations Group to ask which private lab they used. I disappointed him when I said I still wasn't interested in coming back to work with the outfit. He put me on hold and returned with the information. I swabbed my cheek and placed that in a separate bag. Now I needed someone to cart me to the post office so I could box and ship everything.

During Lizzie's house renovation converting it to two condos, she had created a separate exterior entrance for the second-floor condo, where she lived. Inside, she had enclosed the original staircase between the first and second floors and added a door at the top. She, Paddy, or Megan used that stairway to come downstairs. I was fine with them doing it, but if I crutched upstairs and pounded on the door, I'd feel like I was invading Lizzie's privacy.

It's silly, I'm sure, but I felt better hobbling outside and ringing her doorbell. No answer. I checked my voicemail and messages. Nothing. Where was everyone when they should be here getting ready for dinner? Acid burned in my stomach, which since breakfast had had only the mug of water at my mother's. My imagination insisted the FBI must be holding Paddy incommunicado. Lizzie and Megan were somewhere, and she hadn't had time to tell me where. I'd call Paddy's defense attorney—if I knew his name.

Okay, Seamus, start standing on your one leg. You're hungry, feed yourself. I grabbed a yogurt from the fridge and slumped into a chair at the table. Only then did I see the note.

NINE

PADDY AND MEGAN WERE IN the air, flying back to Chicago. He'd call this evening to fill me in on his day. The relief I felt that he wasn't in jail changed to the ache of missing family. I agreed it was best for them to return to wife and mother, but logic did not assuage my heart.

Lizzie had added a postscript to Paddy's note. After seeing them off at the airport, she was meeting friends for drinks, dinner, and retail therapy—her way of dealing with their departure.

"You and me, Peg-leg." I told my reflection in the window. "Let's make this happen."

I called a cab, realizing Paddy and Colleen would have both used a ride app. I was on the wrong side of that electronic divide. I gave the cabbie the address, and he shot me a dirty look in the mirror. "Look," I said. "I know it's a short distance and crawling through rush hour to get to me cost you money. I want you to wait for me at the post office with your meter running—and I tip very well. Okay?"

I didn't catch what he muttered, which might have been a good thing. He turned his radio up, which made it difficult for me to order takeout from a local Chinese place.

Errands completed, I tipped the cabbie, and he was gracious enough to apologize—his old lady was on him because he had left a pen in a shirt pocket and it had ruined a bunch of clothes. He offered to carry the takeout to the door. I could have done it myself, but I thought he'd feel better if I let him be a good guy.

Paddy called while I was eating dinner. He spoke in a rush. "The police wouldn't show my defense attorney the six-pack of mug shots they used for the witness to identify me. He figured something was hinky and told them to charge me or we were leaving. Outside the station, he suggested I go home to Chicago. You and Mom got your wish. We packed up at Mom's, and she took us to the airport. How did your day go?"

I replayed my activities, leaving out how much better I'd have felt if he had called me earlier. "I'll see what Colleen has tomorrow morning. Tonight, I'll search the Happy Reaper's computer files for something I can use for leverage."

"You want help?"

"Not tonight. Spend time with your lovely wife and give her a kiss for me. My dinner's getting cold, Paddy."

I shoveled the food in, never tasting it, and cleaned and shelved the dishes. Nutrition requirements met, I laid a blank piece of paper—to remind me I should have no preconceived notions—on the table and slapped on headphones and dialed up a classical mix of Gershwin, Elgar, and Ravel. Using an encrypted browser, I accessed the copy of the Happy Reaper's hard drive that Paddy had stored in the darknet and followed my nose, clicking from file to file.

Deep into it, a light touch on my shoulder startled me. Lizzie. She said something I didn't hear over strains of the Finale of Elgar's *Enigma Variations*. I pulled off the headphones. "What?"

"See what I bought?" Lizzie spun around in a

diaphanous kimono-style robe. Green vines with delicate yellow flowers scrolled across the material. During the twenty-plus years since our divorce, her breasts had become fuller and her waist thicker, but she was still stunning.

"It's lovely." Embarrassed by my body's stirrings, I returned my focus to her face. "Did the girls like it?"

"Oh, yes. They suggested I show you." She slurred her words. "You like?"

"I talked to Paddy," I said. "He and Megan are home. Fingers crossed that out-of-sight is out-of-mind with the FBI. I doubt it. I'm sure it was hard for you to see them leave."

She looked at the floor, ran her hands down the kimono over her thighs. "You did a good job raising him, Seamus. I was such a shit mother. A shit person."

"Lizzie, I'm hearing alcohol talking. I think you should—"

"I'm talking." She straightened to her full five feet seven inches. "Maybe the alcohol's letting me say things I've wanted to say for a long time. I was wrong about you. I was wrong about Patrick. And I was wrong about us. I was young and foolish and stupid. I want to try again." Her face glowed. "There, I've said it."

As if she controlled my play list, into the silence came the opening notes of Ravel's *Bolero*.

AFTER AN HOUR AND A half conversation, each of us blaming ourselves for our marriage breaking up, a now sober Lizzie returned to her bedroom upstairs. Alone.

I was too wired to fall asleep. If I could find the Happy Reaper's money, I could try to point the Feds in the right direction so they could seize it. Without money, he couldn't pay for an escape or hire someone to kill my family.

Tantalizing clues filled two pages of a legal pad, but unless he was careless or I was lucky, it might take months or years to find his money. My mind wandered, and I jotted notes about how to set up a fake escape attempt and con him into releasing the promised $2.5 million. We could follow that money to his stash. Perfect for a thriller, but the FBI would never go for it.

Around 2:30 I stumbled upon chapter notes the Happy Reaper had made for his memoir. Chief Riley had mentioned he was writing a memoir, and what was clear was how important his legacy was to him. That might give me the leverage I needed.

Or not.

With the Happy Reaper, my track record had not been great.

TEN

SLEEP CAME LATE, THE ALARM came early, and I was groggy when the physical therapist arrived. She and her tight glutes worked me hard. Before leaving, she reminded me that my recovery also required getting enough sleep. As my mother would say, if wishes were horses, beggars would ride. I had fifteen minutes before Colleen arrived. I turned on the shower and the phone rang.

Colleen was making great progress but was running late. She had found another instance of two museums receiving what she suspected were identical documents. Unlike the first two museums we'd found, these welcomed the opportunity to discuss her concerns via a noon conference call.

COLLEEN ARRIVED WITH FOOD IN hand. "You being a guy, I didn't know what you had, and I forgot to eat breakfast." She spread her papers on the table. At high noon she connected us and the two museums on a conference call. One director described the "original letter" he had received and read it. The other director said it matched word for word the document he also had believed was original.

"Shall we try to reach the Grants Administrator and see what he has to say?" I asked. They agreed. Since

Chambers Austin III had accused Colleen of sexual harassment, I made the call with Colleen listening and ready to hand me the evidence.

Telling the receptionist I was interested in donations was all it took to get Aussie to pick up. I introduced the museum directors and indicated we wanted to know the provenance of the documents in question.

He hemmed and hawed, and when he finally formed words, he squeaked like Mickey Mouse. "We can't provide donors' names without their permission. I will make inquiries and get back to the museums once I have information."

"When can we expect that?" the Arkansas museum director asked.

"Got me," Aussie mumbled. "As long as it takes."

Aussie hung up, which allowed Colleen to debrief the two curators. They planned to follow up if they didn't hear anything from him by the end of the week.

The call complete, Colleen said, "So we kicked the hornets' nest. Now what?"

"My son has taught me the power of online searches. Let's put in the name of the soldier who wrote those letters."

Too many results came up, but additional search terms provided an eBay entry in the top spot after the ads. Logging into the platform, we found a collection of forty-eight "Civil War era letters" written by our guy that had sold in auction for $1,200. The auction date was six months before someone had donated similar letters to the museums.

The seller was a Cincinnati, Ohio antiquarian shop. I had browsed that shop while I lived in Cincy and had found its staff friendly. The product page included pictures of the letters. Among them, we found one that matched our suspect letter word for word.

And then I found another online auction: three weeks later with the identical description. Sales price: $58,824. It provided the bidding history. Only one bid, nearly fifty times more than the earlier price.

I called the online auction house, spoke with the manager, and said I had hand-drawn Civil War era maps I wanted to auction. How did their services work? Discounting all the sales crap, the core service cost 15% of the sales price. For that, they received the articles, verified the descriptions were appropriate, handled the auction, collected funds, and shipped the purchased material to the winning bidder. My antenna twitched. For the suspect transaction, the seller received, net of the commission paid on $58,824, a nice round figure of $50,000.

"Do the buyer and seller know each other's identities?"

"No, sir. We keep that information in an online SQL database. Very secure."

I told him I had other firms to contact and thanked him for his time. I called the Cincinnati shop and tried a different approach. "My name is Seamus McCree. I am a financial crimes investigator working on a case regarding forged documents. You sold the documents—the originals, not the forgeries—on eBay." I assured him that we did not think they had done anything dodgy and then gave him all the transactional information we knew. "We hope you can cooperate with this investigation and provide us with the name and address of the person to whom you delivered the packet of letters."

"That is against our policy, sir."

"We could get a warrant, but if we did, we'd expand it

to include any other transactions you may have had with any of the individuals involved. This is much simpler."

He paused, and I let him think. "How do I know to whom I am speaking?"

"I've given you my name. If you do an internet search, you'll see who I am, what I do. A reverse phone number search will show you this number is mine. I can wait while you call me back to assure yourself that I haven't spoofed the number." Generosity is my middle name.

"Let me copy down the information. I need to speak with the owner."

"Please do," I said in my most cooperative voice. "I hope to hear from you soon."

Colleen sprang to her feet and paced the room. "I feel like a juggler with thirty balls in the air waiting for them to all crash on my head."

"Welcome to my world. Consider what we know. The packet sold for twelve hundred bucks. Soon after, the same packet fetched an amount that, after commissions, provided their owner fifty grand." I paused to let the information settle. "If I wanted to give you fifty thousand and not pay gift tax, I might pay you that much for your shoelace. You should pay taxes on the gain, but that's on you, not on me."

"So instead, you buy the letters from me, and I buy them back from you?"

"Close," I said, "but you'd be out the twelve hundred bucks. How about I *give* you the articles and then buy them from you?"

"No gift tax because it's under fifteen grand."

"Bingo. And to increase the tax deduction I claim, I supplement the material by making copies of the letters.

You were right to suspect fraud. You've done a great job. Keep digging to find similar transactions. I have another matter to take care of tomorrow, but I promise I'll continue to dissect the financials."

And I need to talk with Paddy because he has skills I do not.

ELEVEN

THE COUNTY JAIL HOUSING THE Happy Reaper used a large open room for the normal Thursday visitation. Prisoners and their visitors sat in folding chairs, huddled together in twos and threes. Two guards cruised the room while others stood along the walls and on both sides of the doors. The Happy Reaper's wheelchair provided his seat. My crutches were still a security issue. I hopped on my good leg, supporting myself on the folding chair I pushed across the floor to position it in front of his wheelchair.

"Zoo time," the Happy Reaper said, "and I get my own stork."

"Your lucky day," I said. "You wanted something to trade and I've got it. I know you're preparing an autobiography and—"

"Memoir, not autobiography. There's a difference."

"Right, one tells the truth and the other covers up the—"

His eyes flashed anger. "That's not it. An autobiography covers the chronology of a life. A memoir focuses on one particular aspect."

"Becoming and being the Happy Reaper. Got it. Thing is, I am the one person who knows intimate details of your failures. I'm willing to shop those details to *The National Enquirer* or some other rag sheet that would love the inside skinny. Your mugshot on the front page. Headline shouting *Happy Reaper Depressed Over Failures.* Details on how I stopped you from killing a hundred nuns, how last month a photographer—a young woman—took you down. Stuff like that. No one will believe your memoir."

His mouth formed a grim line. His eyes pinched into malevolent slits. He gripped the wheelchair's arms so hard his hands turned bone white. Without the chains, he might have tried to strangle me.

"Or," I said. "we can agree to a deal. You leave my family and friends alone and I won't interfere with your memoir."

He smiled. "No interference from any McCree. Or friend."

My muscles relaxed in relief. Pricking his pride, not letting him keep the facade that he was the best hit man in the country, was the leverage I needed to strike the bargain. "I'll put it in writing."

"Yeah," he grumbled. "That would be worth something."

Don't oversell, just close the deal. "So—"

"So." His face brightened. "Damned good try. Makes me proud of you, and I'll feel even better when it's published. Who are they going to believe, a sour-grapes guy or the Happy Reaper providing intimate details behind his greatest hits—so to speak?"

He threw his head back and laughed. Under his breath he said, "Nice try, loser."

I choked down my fury at being stymied by his ego, or maybe worse, by his being right. Footsteps sounded behind me. Was a guard reacting to my expression? I followed the noise to discover it came from a prisoner and guard about to pass us on their way to the exit. Returning my attention to the Happy Reaper, I blew out a stream of air.

Clear your mind. Bank the fire of your anger. There must be something he wants. Swallow your pride and ask.

From the corner of my eye I caught a blur of motion flicking past the Happy Reaper. The world slowed down, a feeling I remembered from playing soccer. In my playing days, I saw the spin of the ball in exquisite detail, anticipated its bounce, knew precisely each player's moves.

Now, a spurt of blood from the Happy Reaper's severed carotid arced to the ceiling, splattering the acoustical tiles. The prisoner continued nonchalantly walking. His guard was unaware of the assault. The Happy Reaper's hand spasmed toward the gaping slash in his neck. His eyes grew wide with surprise. His mouth opened to shout.

In the beat before the second eruption of hot blood, an unworthy thought registered. No doubt triggered by Chief Riley's throwaway comment on how easy things would be if the Happy Reaper died, a little voice suggested this was a gift. I could let him die.

Without a moment of internal debate, I curled my good foot underneath the chair and launched myself onto the Happy Reaper. I clamped both hands over his wound and felt a pulse of hot blood cover my hands and stream down my arms.

Yelling filled my ears. Maybe it was me.

The Happy Reaper bucked against me, dislodging my grip, allowing the third spurt to catch me full in the face, blinding me. His only chance was for me to apply firm pressure until a guard trained to deal with this kind of trauma could take charge. I blinked away the blood and slid my left hand up his neck, felt the roughness of the wound with my thumb, and moved my palm over the gash. With my right hand, I grabbed the back of the left, leaned in, and pressed hard.

A lifetime later, strong hands flung me to the floor, pulled my arms behind me, and cuffed my wrists.

THE WORST PART OF SPENDING hours in police custody was wearing blood-soaked clothes. The hot blood cooled and dried, leaving me chilled. Adrenaline dissipated, and I shivered until they covered me with a blanket.

Every time I closed my eyes, the arc of the Happy Reaper's blood appeared. The metallic stench of spilled blood filled my every breath.

A guard remembered that during my first visit I had threatened to contact the Irish mob and put a contract on John Smith. My claim that this attacker was black didn't seem to carry any weight until they reviewed videotape from cameras monitoring the visitation room. One camera caught the flash of a shiv as the prisoner walked by and proved I'd tried to save the Happy Reaper, not kill him.

At that point they became concerned for my health. A check of their records showed the Happy Reaper's blood carried no infectious diseases—no surprise to me since he kept himself in excellent physical condition. They carted me to hospital emergency to x-ray my ankle, which now throbbed with angry pain. I'd be sore for a while, but all the pins holding it together were in place. When the cops discovered I had taken a cab from Cambridge to Leominster, they insisted on driving me home to Lizzie's.

Sitting in the plastic rear seat of the police car, I checked my phone for messages. One from Chief Riley ("What the hell are you up to, Seamus?"), several from Lizzie asking if I was okay, and one from Colleen. Her message said someone had posted on YouTube a cellphone video of me saving the Happy Reaper's life. It had gone viral.

I watched the video and heard people screaming, felt my blood pressure rise, saw my hands had stopped the blood spurts. Seconds later, a cop wrestled me to the ground and threw himself on top of me. My ankle throbbed with each beat of my heart. One more gush of blood erupted from the Happy Reaper's neck as the guards shifted him to a gurney and rushed him from the room.

I hardly had enough energy to press the button and retrieve the final phone message.

It was from the Cincinnati antiquarian shop. C. Austin with a post office box in Newburyport, Massachusetts bought the bundle of correspondence. He recited Austin's email address: letters and numbers with no discernible meaning.

I searched the Internet for the email address and arrived at an abandoned LinkedIn account for Chambers Austin, Jr. The chairman of the board of Harpoon Services was going down, but I needed more information.

At Lizzie's, I removed my clothes inside the door and sealed them in a garbage bag. I cranked the shower to maximum heat and scrubbed blood off my skin, out of my hair, and from under my nails. Feeling chilled when I finished, I dressed in heavy sweats and crawled under the covers. From the bed, I called Paddy. "FBI leaving you alone?"

"So far. Any luck with the information Colleen gave you?"

I brought him up to speed on my discoveries. Through the connection came the clicking of a keyboard. "This from the Franklin, Howe and Howe server: an email to Hodkin Stuart, the Harpoon account partner-in-charge, from c.austin.jr@harpoonenergy.org dated Monday last week. It reads, quote CC still digging. I need this stopped. If you can't, I will use the nuclear option. End quote. The response was quote, use private email for this, end quote."

"CC has to be Colleen Carpetti," I said, "It's suggestive but not conclusive that the two of them hatched a plan to force her out with the bogus sexual harassment claim. I wonder if they decided on that charge because it's in all the news or because one of them was familiar with it."

"I have an idea, Dad. Let me try something. I'll call you back."

Warmed for the moment, I got out of bed. I had work to do before Colleen showed up early the next morning.

TWELVE

THE ALARM WOKE ME FIFTEEN minutes before Colleen's scheduled 6:30 arrival. To jumpstart my brain after only three hours' sleep, I chugged two diet Dr Peppers and downed a painkiller to control my ankle's discomfort.

I led Colleen to the table where I had laid out the evidence. "Exhibit one," I pointed. "At least two women have filed sexual harassment suits against Chambers Austin, Jr. One here in Boston, the other in D.C. Exhibit two: both women used the same online auction house to sell historical documents to Chambers Austin, Jr. They—"

"How do we know this, Seamus?"

Despite my injunctions to the contrary, Paddy had gone hacking. "The information is in a database that's part of the auction company's website. I don't understand how it works, but Paddy used what he called a SQL injection to access a database that contained the names and addresses of both buyers and sellers of all the firm's online auctions. In both cases Chambers bought the documents from a single source. We believe he gifted them to his victims and then bought them back. That's how he paid them to drop their lawsuits. Then, he used Harpoon to facilitate his donations to various historical societies, which allowed him to claim exorbitant tax deductions. You, me, and every other taxpayer subsidized his payoffs."

"So, we've got him?"

I shook my head. "We can't use the database information because we got it illegally. The only way this works is to get one of the two women to talk to us and confirm what we suspect. They probably signed nondisclosure agreements. But, if you meet them in person, maybe they'll confirm our suspicions. According to her online profiles, the local one was doing a summer internship with Chambers' firm. She's an accounting senior at Babson College."

Her eyes shown with determination. "What have I got to lose?"

"Take Lizzie with you. She's empathetic when she wants to be and can serve as an independent witness. But don't tell her about this." I waved to the material covering the table. "She'd be furious if she knew Paddy was still hacking."

FAME MAY LAST ONLY FIFTEEN minutes but being the top of one news cycle was enough to get me a late afternoon meeting with Gerald Scigliano, the managing partner of Franklin, Howe and Howe. He led me from the door of his office to a round conference table graced with a pot of miniature mums. Settling in, I commented on the unusual decoration.

"I have a black thumb, but my mother is a gardener and insists on bringing me plants. Thank goodness my assistant can keep them alive. I had to ban the scented ones. Some people had negative reactions, like they do to perfume. I'm sure you didn't come here for gardening advice. What can we help you with?"

"I checked you out, as I suspect you did me. You became managing partner at forty and in the thirteen years since, you tripled the firm's size to five hundred employees. We both grew up working class. Me, poor Irish. You, hardscrabble Italian. The most respect you could show someone in my neighborhood was telling them the truth to their face. I hope you're good with that, because unless you do the right thing, you'll destroy Franklin, Howe and Howe."

He cranked his head back and forth, the cracking of his neck loud enough for me to hear. He folded his hands on the desk and leaned forward. "I'm all ears."

"Hodkin Stuart is a cancer you must cut from your company. He's covering up tax fraud, helping hide a client's payoffs to deal with sexual harassment, and he caused you to fire an employee on trumped-up charges."

"Colleen Carpetti, right? Just a minute." He used his intercom and told his assistant to reschedule his next appointment and have Hodkin Stuart join him in his office. "I heard rumors she was consulting a lawyer to contest her dismissal."

Good. One of Colleen's "friends" had talked with management. I had not expected he would bring in Stuart. While we waited, I cautioned myself to be professional, to not let it be personal.

The bastard walked in looking regal: polished fingernails, two-thousand-dollar suit, five-hundred-dollar haircut.

"Have a seat, Hodkin. This is Seamus McCree. He claims to have information you might want to hear firsthand."

Confusion painted Stuart's face. He remained standing. "Who is this guy?"

I thought, "Your biggest nightmare." I said, "A financial crimes investigator representing various parties aggrieved by you."

"Carpetti, right? I don't have time for this crap."

"You do," Scigliano said in a calm voice. "Sit. Mister McCree, you were about to say?"

Stuart pulled a seat out and sat away from the table. He reminded me of a cobra watching a flute player, waiting for a chance to strike. I played prosecutor, presenting exhibit after exhibit, evidence proving Chambers Austin, Junior was a serial sexual predator who had paid numerous women to make allegations go away.

He used online auctions as a mechanism to "buy" merchandise from the victims at exorbitant prices, then donated that material first to Harpoon Services to get a tax deduction. He instructed Harpoon to donate the documents to museums. Even that had not been enough for him: he'd created forgeries to allow him to double the deduction.

"This is total bullshit." A flush colored Stuart's face and a ring of sweat showed under his arms. "Why would a guy worth billions stoop to this shit?"

"Greed," I said. "Now we come to you, Stuart. You covered up the accounting fraud. When Colleen unearthed the tip of the iceberg, you conspired with Austin Junior and Austin the Third to have her fired. Ironically, you concocted a sexual harassment allegation—something Junior has experience with. In fact, the complaint against Colleen was virtually a carbon copy of one lodged against Junior."

Stuart flew to his feet. "That is complete and utter bullshit. Why are you listening to this crap, Gerry?" To me he said, "I'll sue your ass from here to the Vineyard."

"Sit, Hodkin." Scigliano waited until he had. "Assuming you have evidence to back up your claims," he pointed to the pile of papers before me, "what do you propose?"

"First, Stuart resigns his partnership at FHH. Should he wish to protect his name, he will donate his partnership equity to a charity that assists people who have suffered sexual harassment, regardless of age, sex, or orientation."

"This is a complete fabrication." Spittle flew from Stuart's mouth, staining the front of his starched shirt. "Carpetti got caught, and we dealt with her as we should. Now this scumbag is trying to bribe us into letting her back. What message would that send? He's—"

"Do you know," I said, "Colleen Carpetti is a lesbian? Been out since high school?"

His dropped jaw said he had not known.

"That's true?" Scigliano asked. "Why didn't she say so?" His head dropped. A moment later he regained control of his emotions. "Because we bulldozed her. If you were in my position, Mr. McCree, what would you do?"

"Offer Colleen Carpetti her job back. I don't know whether she'll accept. Regardless, hold an all-employee meeting and tell everyone that Hodkin Stuart manufactured the reasons for her termination and is no longer a member of the firm. Furthermore, FHH will assist in Chambers Austin, Junior's criminal prosecution and in any civil suit Colleen files against him and his son."

"Help me understand something, Mr. McCree. Why are you doing this? What's your relation to Colleen?"

I couldn't answer the question regarding my relationship with Colleen, but the fires of justice burned inside me. "I despise predators. Financial predators. Sexual Predators. Those who use their positions of power to repress the people we grew up with. With what I know here, how could I live with myself if I did anything less than take on these men?"

"Hodkin," Scigliano said, "you have until first thing Monday morning to resign should you choose. Stay or leave as you like. Mr. McCree, show me you're right."

THIRTEEN

I RETURNED FROM THE FHH meeting to Lizzie's and found her running a vacuum over spotless floors. Under cover of the tornado, I crutched inside the house, leaned against the wall and used fingers to plug my ears.

She saw me and killed power to the infernal beast.

"You should wear earplugs when you run that thing," I said.

"What?" She cupped her hands at her ears, a grin giving away the joke. "You got mail. What's in the package?" Lizzie held out a thick envelope stamped CONFIDENTIAL.

I took the envelope. "Aren't you going to ask how the meeting went?"

"Your mile-wide grin told me they believed the information Colleen and I got from that sweet girl we met this morning."

"Let's go to a nice restaurant and celebrate. Stuart is toast. FHH will reinstate Colleen if she wants it. It will take time and effort, but the Austins are going down for the count. I'll have Colleen contact the IRS so she can become eligible for payment under their whistleblower award program."

"Seamus, why are you hiding the envelope behind your back?"

"Didn't you see it said Confidential?"

"I didn't open it. Does it show whether Colleen is your daughter? She's the right age for your time with—what was her name? Rachel? Raquel? Randy? Something like that. Two weeks right before you graduated?"

I collapsed into the chair. Rachelle. I had forgotten her. And Lizzie was right, it hadn't lasted two weeks. The envelope seemed hotter and heavier than it had moments ago. Good Lord, Colleen *could* be my kid. Here I'd convinced myself that she was my sister Ailish's kid or, less likely, a late love child of my mother's. Mine?

"You going to open it?"

"No. I'm not."

She reached for it. "I'll do it for you if you're chicken."

I pulled it away. "You know I want to know. The results are what they are, but they're not for me. I'm giving this to Colleen. It's hers to open or hold or burn. It's her life, not mine."

"Jesus," Lizzie said. "You've grown up."

Before I realized it, she was in my lap and we were necking like teenagers.

BY THE TIME LIZZIE AND I untangled and I reached Colleen, we were smack dab in Cambridge's peak Friday night dining-out rush. Colleen suggested EVOO, a Cambridge restaurant serving sustainably produced local food. Our reservation was for 9:30. The waitress led us to Colleen, seated at the table, sipping a sparkling water.

"A hundred bucks says she's your kid," Lizzie whispered in my ear.

"Not a word," I said.

I was bursting at the seams to tell her what happened with FHH, but Colleen asked about my meeting with the

Happy Reaper. While we waited for our meals, I relived the awful scene of blood shooting from his neck.

"Do they know," she asked, "why the guy tried to kill him?"

"I talked with Chief Riley today. His sources suggest the inmate had a beef because he thought the Happy Reaper had disrespected him. We may never know for sure. Let me tell you what happened at FHH."

The meals arrived. I had a combination of foods I would never have paired. I think it was good, but I was too nervous to taste anything. Between bites, I related Gerry Scigliano's reactions to the information I gave him implicating his crooked partner. "Do you plan to go back to work with them?"

"I'll talk with Gerry. I have to say our amateur sleuthing was a lot more fun than straight accounting."

"Probably doesn't pay as well," I said.

"Seamus," Lizzie said, "you are not one to speak against doing what you love, not what pays the best."

For the rest of the meal, the women chatted up a storm, feeling no need to include me. Fine with me. My thoughts centered on what Colleen would do with the envelope burning a hole in my knapsack. I waited until the women ordered coffee before presenting Colleen the envelope along with my explanation of how I had obtained the DNA samples. "The results are here, if you still want them."

Colleen folded her napkin and squared it to the table's edge. "What's it say?"

"I don't know." I gave it a nudge. "Maybe I shouldn't have done it, but I thought you wanted to know. It's not an excuse, but Lizzie reminded me—" How could I tell her I might be her father but had forgotten the woman who would then be her mother? "It turns out it's possible I could be your father. Regardless, the information is yours, not mine."

"You know, the Carpettis will always be my parents."

"As they should be," I said and believed.

We fiddled with our water glasses. The longer Colleen remained silent, the more dinner felt like a lead weight in my stomach. I'd screwed up again, starting this because I wanted to know, not considering whether Colleen really did. I tingled with curiosity, but I'd like her regardless of her parentage.

"Seamus," Colleen said, "I haven't known you long, but if I had a second father, I think you'd be a terrific one." She inserted her finger into the flap, sawed it across the seal, and pulled out the thick bundle. From my seat, the top page looked like a cover letter. I didn't try my trick of reading upside down. I tracked the movement of her eyes.

They wove back and forth, followed the lines down the page. Her body still as stone. She finished reading, slid the pages into the envelope, and tucked it into the cute leather carryall I had liked so much the first time I saw it.

Emotions played on her face, but I couldn't read them. Would she keep it to herself? Oh man, I had told myself I was okay not knowing, but that was when no one knew. I exhaled a long breath and startled Colleen.

"I am surprised," she said. "I was sure I knew the answer. Please give me a moment."

Never had sixty seconds taken so long.

"I'm your . . ." She smiled and shook her head. "I'm your sister. Half-sister."

So, it was Mom. I searched Colleen's face for evidence of either of the men I thought might be her father, but I still couldn't find any similarities. That was why I had leaned toward Colleen being my sister's daughter—at least until Lizzie pointed out I could have been the father.

"Do you—" Colleen's voice caught. "Do you know why? Why she gave me up for adoption?"

And this, I realized, was a downside I had not considered. I suppose every adopted child wonders why her mother gave her up. It's one thing to speculate in a vacuum and something different once you discover who your mother is. "I suspect the only living person who knows is my—our mother. You'll have to ask her, and to be honest, I doubt she'll tell you."

If Colleen had been the one to request the DNA testing, I would be blameless. But I should have known most people would succumb to curiosity. Wasn't that the story of Adam, Eve, and the apple? I was the damn snake. Colleen's hand on my arm brought me back from my concerns.

"Thank you for doing this. You're right. I wanted to know. I was sure you were my father, and I worried you'd think I was trying to get something from you if I asked you to take a paternity test. Will it be okay with you if we don't tell your mother right away?"

"I mean it, Colleen. The information is yours."

FOURTEEN

OUR DINNER BROKE UP SOON after. Too little sleep and too much emotion had drained my reserves. I needed time alone to recharge and consider everything that had happened. Lizzie remained quiet on the way home, which allowed my thoughts to bubble. Colleen seemed to have taken the news well, but there could still be blowback from my decision to test our DNA. So far, the FBI hadn't made any more moves. But just like the Happy Reaper's threat, all these things were hanging over my head, over the heads of the entire McCree clan.

In a stroke of luck, Lizzie had to wait for a Mercedes Benz to vacate the parking space in front of her house. Under her breath she murmured, "Clean living."

Her clean living, not mine. She parallel parked on the first try. "Good thing you're driving," I said. "It would take me four tries and I'd run over the curb at least once."

"Ah yes, the famous Seamus McCree school of parallel parking: obliterate the flowerbed but end up perfectly parked." She opened the passenger door and helped me out. "That's the story of your life, isn't it?"

"You're saying it's easy being me?"

"Oh God no. I can't imagine how hard it is to be an opinionated curmudgeon who sticks his nose in everyone's business, and yet everyone still loves you.

Don't you look at me like I'm crazy. This is me talking." She slapped me on the shoulder, causing me to stumble. "Sorry. Forgot. I had only one glass of wine tonight. And—"

"What's on your porch?" I stopped and pointed to a package. Red paper, white bow the size of a baseball, it sat centered before the door to the downstairs unit. I thought of the Mercedes that had conveniently vacated the parking spot in front of Lizzie's house. Was it the one that had followed Colleen? That was—

"Stop changing the subject, Seamus. I want us to give us a second try. You've got a long time to recuperate. Stay with me. No one has to know."

No more family secrets! Wait. That's your first thought, Seamus? Not, *this will never work.* Focus on the package.

Nobody who knew I was in Cambridge would leave a wrapped package on the doorstep. Anyone giving Lizzie a present knew she lived upstairs. Unless Lizzie had arranged it—a key to the upstairs?

"Is this from you?"

"Don't be ridiculous. I've been with you the whole time." She marched ahead of me to the porch.

Which didn't answer the question. "Wait, Lizzie." Dread filled me and I wondered why.

"For Pete's sake." She held the package to the light. "The tag says Seamus A. McCree with this address. It's nippy out, let's get inside."

A package on the porch. A Mercedes leaving at our arrival. Gray? Like the one that had maybe followed Colleen? I picked up my pace. For no good reason, I didn't want to bring it inside. Colleen's paranoia was catching. "Wait. Let me open it."

"For Pete's sake, Seamus. You can't sprint on crutches. I'll wait." She made the sign of the cross.

I grabbed the package from her and removed the bow, shoving it in my pocket. I pried up an edge of tape and ripped the wrapping with my teeth, uncovering a Rolex watch box. Shaking it told me nothing. Lifting its cover, my heart sank. Inside was the Happy Reaper's business card, Celtic Cross side up.

He'd learned where I was. He had people outside doing his bidding. I flipped the card and held it under the light. Black ink lined out the "Results Guaranteed." Underneath in precise printing was *Thanks for saving me. Mano a mano it is.*

I hope you enjoyed reading this story. To help me reach other readers, I would appreciate your posting a short review of *Furthermore* on your favorite retailer or review website.

Author's Note

THIS NOVELLA OWES ITS BIRTH to readers who insisted that the next novel in the series had to return to the Boston area and address a question I left open at the end of *False Bottom*. The problem for me was that I planned for the "G" novel to take place up at the McCree camp in Michigan's Upper Peninsula. This novella was created through that tension.

I enjoy visiting potential story locations in person, but for this novella I had to rely on previous visits to the Greater Boston area and Google. I have not been in or around any Leominster, Massachusetts jails and prisons. I relied on research visits I've made to other jails and prisons and conversations over the years with Jon Olson, a retired prison guard, to create fictional settings that worked for the story. Any resemblance to the real facilities is pure luck.

Linda Gorchels, Tracey Kathryn, and Janet Schrader, members with me in the Wisconsin Chapter of Sisters in Crime, read an early draft and made many helpful suggestions. David Leach read an even earlier draft to try to prevent me from perverting Boston geography and language choices. My two eagle-eyed readers, Carol J. Baldridge and Dottie Caster prevented me from committing many abuses of the English language. Jan Rubens is always my first, last, and best reader.

My name is on the cover and the mistakes that remain are attributable to me. I love to hear from readers. Drop me a note and let me know how you liked the story or that you found a typo so I can correct it for future editions. My email is jmj@jamesmjackson.com.

James M. Jackson
Amasa, Michigan

James M. Jackson authors the Seamus McCree series.

Jim has also published an acclaimed book on contract bridge, *One Trick at a Time: How to start winning at bridge.*

He calls the deep woods of Michigan's Upper Peninsula home. You can find out more about Jim or sign up for his Readers Group newsletter at his website, https://jamesmjackson.com.